Dear Parent:
Your child's love of reading starts here!

Every child learns to read in a different ~~way~~ ... ed. You can help your young reader improve ... by encouraging his or her own interests a ... guide your child's spiritual development by read ... with biblical values and Bible stories, like I Can Read! books published by Zonderkidz. From books your child reads with you to the first books he or she reads alone, there are I Can Read! books for every stage of reading:

SHARED READING
Basic language, word repetition, and whimsical illustrations, ideal for sharing with your emergent reader.

BEGINNING READING
Short sentences, familiar words, and simple concepts for children eager to read on their own.

READING WITH HELP
Engaging stories, longer sentences, and language play for developing readers.

READING ALONE
Complex plots, challenging vocabulary, and high-interest topics for the independent reader.

ADVANCED READING
Short paragraphs, chapters, and exciting themes for the perfect bridge to chapter books.

I Can Read! books have introduced children to the joy of reading since 1957. Featuring award-winning authors and illustrators and a fabulous cast of beloved characters, I Can Read! books set the standard for beginning readers.

A lifetime of discovery begins with the magical words **"I Can Read!"**

Visit www.icanread.com for information on enriching your child's reading ...
Visit www.zonderkidz.com for more Zonderkidz I Can Read! title.

God saw all that he had made,
and it was very good ...
—Genesis 1:31

ZONDERKIDZ

Bob and Larry's Creation Vacation
Copyright © 2011 Big Idea Entertainment, LLC. VEGGIETALES®, character
names, likenesses and other indicia are trademarks of and copyrighted by Big Idea
Entertainment, LLC. All rights reserved.
Illustrations © 2011 by Big Idea Entertainment, Inc.

Requests for information should be addressed to:
Zonderkidz, Grand Rapids, Michigan 49530

ISBN 978-0-310-72731-6

Editor: Mary Hassinger
Art direction: Karen Poth
Cover design: Karen Poth
Interior design: Ron Eddy

'rinted in China

ZONDERkidz

I Can Read!

BEGINNING READING 1

Bob and Larry's Creation Vacation

story by Karen Poth

Bob and Larry love to go on vacation.

This year, Larry has planned

a special trip.

"We are going
to see all of
God's creation!"
Larry told Bob.
The two friends
looked at a map.

"We can't do that," Bob said.

"We don't have enough time."

"Sure we do," Larry said.

"We only need seven days!

Pack your bags," Larry said.

"We leave in the morning!"

"On the first day,

God made the light," Larry said.

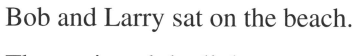

Bob and Larry sat on the beach.

They enjoyed the light.

It was a good day!

"Later on that same day," Larry said, "God made the night." Larry turned out the light.

Then Larry started to snore.

It was a better night for Larry

than for Bob!

"On the second day," Larry said,

"God made the sky!"

Bob and Larry flew

like birds in the sky!

It was a good day!

"On the third day," Larry said,

"God made the blue sea!"

Bob and Larry swam in the ocean.

It was a good day!

"Then later, on that same day,"

Larry said, "God made the land."

"It is good to be on land!"

Bob said, happy to be out of the water.

"On the fourth day,"
Larry said,
"God hung the sun,
moon, and stars."

"They give the world more sparkle,

don't you think, Bob?"

Larry asked.

It was a good day!

"On the fifth day," Larry said,

"God made the fish

in the water."

"And the birds in the air!" Bob said,

as a pelican picked him up

and flew away.

It was NOT a good bird!

"God made more than

10,000 kinds of birds," Larry said,

"and more than 28,000

kinds of fish!"

God worked hard on day five!

It was a good day!

"On the sixth day,"
Larry said,
"God made the creatures
on the land."

"All of them," Bob said,

"from the littlest ant

to the biggest elephant!"

"Think about all the creatures

God made that day!" Larry said.

"Bugs and rabbits, turtles and deer,

beetles and mice, starfish and owls."

"And later that same day," said Larry, "God made man and woman."

"He named them Adam and Eve!" Bob said.

It was a good day!

On the seventh day,

Bob and Larry were tired!

They had seen all that God created.

So just like God, they decided to rest!

It was a GREAT vacation!

And God saw everything
that he had made, and,
behold, it was very good.